MARDI GRAS

REVISED AND UPDATED

Dianne M. MacMillan

Enslow Elementary

an imprint of

Enslow Publishers, Inc.

40 Industrial Road
Box 398
Berkeley Heights, NJ 07922
USA

http://www.enslow.com

To my husband, Jim, who shared Mardi Gras with me.

Enslow Elementary, an imprint of Enslow Publishers, Inc.

Enslow Elementary® is a registered trademark of Enslow Publishers, Inc.

Library of Congress Cataloging-in-Publication Data

MacMillan, Dianne M., 1943–
   Mardi Gras / Dianne M. MacMillan. — 2nd ed.
     p. cm. — (Best holiday books)
   Summary: "Read about Mardi Gras and see how it is celebrated in the United States and around the world"—Provided by publisher.
   Includes bibliographical references and index.
   ISBN-13: 978-0-7660-3062-6
   ISBN-10: 0-7660-3062-8
   1. Carnival—Juvenile literature. 2. Carnival—United States—Juvenile literature.
I. Title.
GT4180.M33 2008
394.25—dc22

                               2007002422

To Our Readers: We have done our best to make sure all Internet Addresses in this book were active and appropriate when we went to press. However, the author and the publisher have no control over and assume no liability for the material available on those Internet sites or on other Web sites they may link to. Any comments or suggestions can be sent by e-mail to comments@enslow.com or to the address on the back cover.

Contents

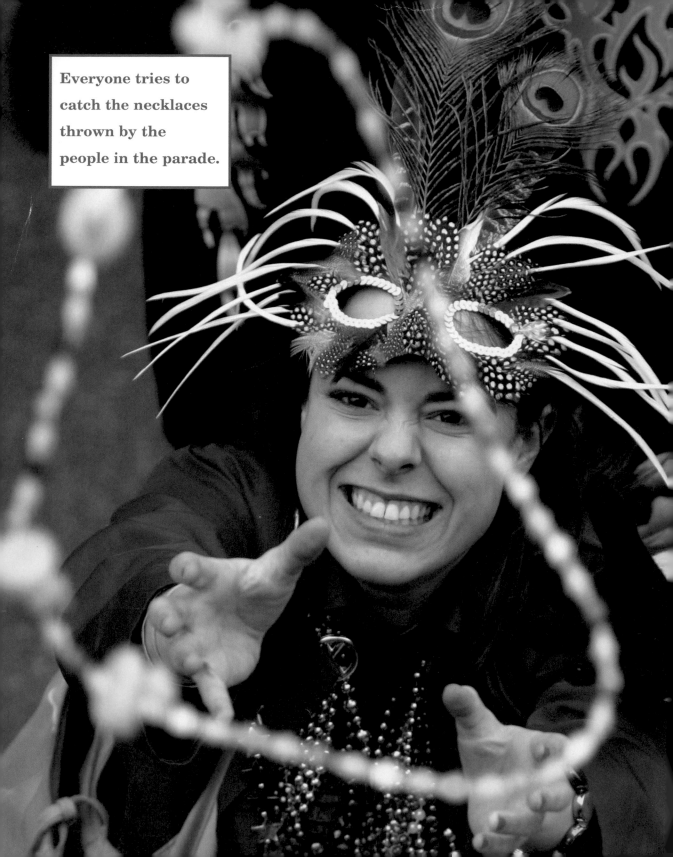

Everyone tries to catch the necklaces thrown by the people in the parade.

A SPECIAL TUESDAY

"THROW ME SOMETHING! THROW ME SOMETHING! Mister, throw me something!" Thousands of people with outstretched arms shout to the passing floats. The beautiful floats decorated with gold-leaf paper roll slowly down the street. People ride on the floats. They wear colorful costumes and masks. Plastic-bead necklaces and pretend gold coins whirl through the air. The masked

The floats in a Mardi Gras parade are all part of a theme, or story. Each parade has a different theme, so no two floats are ever the same!

float riders, called maskers, toss the beads to the crowd. Women, men, and children reach to grab the beads. Singing, shouting, and music are everywhere.

Many in the crowd are dressed up as Gypsies, gorillas, showgirls, skeletons, cowboys, and more. Some

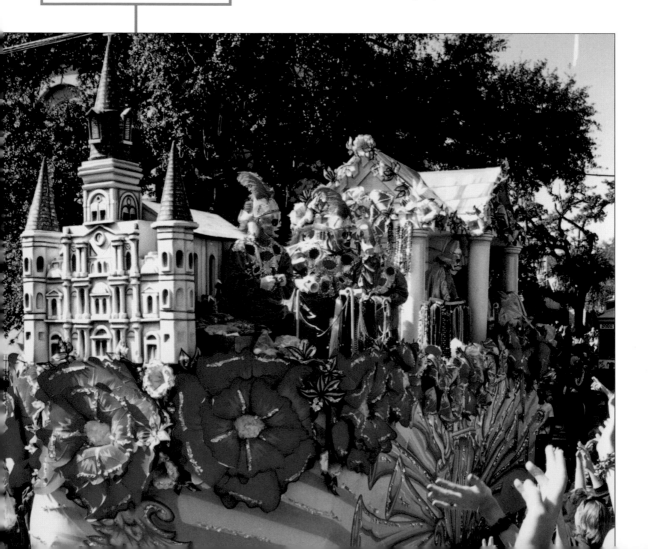

people play Dixieland music on trumpets and clarinets. Others dance behind the musicians. Everyone is celebrating a special Tuesday holiday. It began hundreds of years ago in France. It is like New Year's Eve and Halloween all mixed together. This is Mardi Gras (MAR-dee GRA).

Each year in some cities across the United States people celebrate Mardi Gras. In the southern United States along the Gulf Coast,

> Mardi Gras is like New Year's Eve and Halloween all mixed together.

Mardi Gras can be traced back to 1703. The French first settled in this part of our country. They brought the Mardi Gras holiday with them. Mardi Gras is a three-hundred-year-old tradition in cities like Mobile, Alabama; Galveston, Texas; and New Orleans, Louisiana.

Let's find out more about this joyful celebration.

People used to parade an ox through the streets on Fat Tuesday because they would not be eating meat for forty days.

HOW MARDI GRAS BEGAN

LONG AGO THERE WERE MANY CELEBRATIONS that welcomed spring. People celebrated in hopes that their animals and crops would be plentiful in the coming season. Mardi Gras was part of the spring festival in France. Mardi Gras means "Fat Tuesday." During the celebration, the people paraded a fat ox down the street.

For hundreds of years, Mardi Gras has been celebrated on the Tuesday before Ash

According to Christian tradition, the Wise Men came with gifts for the baby Jesus on January 6th. That is the start of the carnival season.

Wednesday. Ash Wednesday is the first day of Lent. Lent is the six weeks of time before the Christian holiday of Easter. For many years, Christians did not eat meat, cheese, eggs, or butter during Lent. They fasted, which means they ate no food or only small amounts. Knowing that they would soon be fasting, the days before Lent became a time of feasting and partying.

In England, the day before Lent was called Pancake Tuesday. People made stacks and stacks of pancakes. They stopped cooking when all of the eggs and butter and milk were gone. In Germany, the day was called Fastnacht (Eve of Fast). The people baked special rectangular doughnuts. The doughnuts were filled with molasses. Then the doughnuts were dunked in tea.

The French and Spanish called the days before Lent "carnival." The word comes from the Latin words "carne" and "vale," which means "farewell meat." Carnival season begins on January 6, or Twelfth Night. It is the twelfth night after Christmas. Christians believe that the Wise Men or Three Kings brought gifts to the baby Jesus on this day.

Carnival is filled with parties and parades. Each week there are more and more activities until finally the season ends with the joyous, merrymaking day of Mardi Gras. Every year the date of Mardi Gras is different. It can fall on any Tuesday from February 3 to March 9. But it is always forty-six days before Easter.

"Carnival" comes from the Latin words "carne" and "vale," meaning "farewell meat."

In 1699, French explorers landed at the mouth of the Mississippi River. The date was March 3. They set up camp on the river's west bank. Back in France,

Joe Cain dressed up as the fictional "Chief Slacabamorinico" for Mardi Gras. He helped start the tradition of Mardi Gras parades in Mobile, Alabama.

their country was celebrating Mardi Gras. The leader named their camp Pointe du Mardi Gras (Point of Mardi Gras). Three years later, the French founded a settlement near present-day Mobile, Alabama. The first Mardi Gras celebration took place in Mobile. The people held a party, or ball. They wore costumes and masks. Everyone danced just as they had done in France.

In 1718, the French founded the town of Nouvelle Orleans (New Orleans) in what is now Louisiana. French settlers loved the Mardi Gras celebration. They looked forward to the grand masked balls each year. From the early beginnings in Mobile and New Orleans, Mardi Gras has grown and changed.

SECRET CLUBS AND PARADES

In 1857, six young men in New Orleans formed a special carnival club. They called their club the "Mistick Krewe of Comus." Comus was a Roman god of partying in mythology. The men that founded the club paraded on Mardi Gras night with two floats that year. They wore costumes and masks. Servants carried torches and walked alongside the floats. The people of New Orleans were delighted.

This illustration from 1867 shows a "Mistick Krewe of Comus" parade.

The club became known as Comus. The members invented the word "krewe" to stand for their secret club. They also began the tradition of calling a krewe after a name from mythology. Having a parade with floats became a new part of the holiday.

Other people wanted to form secret krewes. Soon there were krewes called

Twelfth Night Revelers, Rex, Momus, and Proteus. In the beginning, the krewe members were only men. Later women formed their own krewes. Some krewes have both men and women members. The Krewe of Little Rascals in New Orleans is made up of boys and girls, ages five to sixteen. Today there are more than one hundred krewes in New Orleans. Some members belong to more than one krewe.

Today there are more than one hundred krewes in New Orleans.

Many other cities have krewes. People in Mobile call their secret clubs "mystic societies." There are more than fifty mystic societies. New ones are formed every year.

Many times the identity of the members is kept secret. Sometimes membership in a krewe is passed down from father to son. The krewe members spend the year planning the parties and parades for next year's Mardi Gras celebration.

During the carnival season, each krewe gives a fancy ball. There is music and dancing. Men dress in tuxedos, and women wear long evening gowns. The

These women are part of a play put on by the Krewe of King Arthur in 2007.

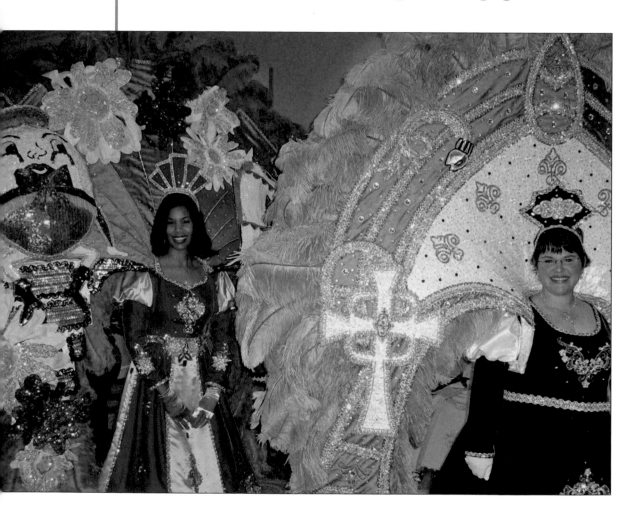

guests wear elaborate masks. In some cities, the guests wear costumes to the ball. Often a king and queen are chosen at the ball. They will reign over the parade and ride in a special float.

Many krewes entertain their guests at the ball by putting on plays. These plays, called tableaus (TAB-lohs), show scenes from history or legends. The themes of the tableaus are kept secret until the ball. Guests look forward to watching these plays.

Many of the balls are private. Only krewe members and their guests are invited. But the parades are for everyone. During carnival season, each krewe parades on different streets on an assigned day. Some krewes parade in the daytime, others at night. Sometimes there are as many as seventy parades within a few

> Many krewes entertain their ball guests with plays showing scenes from history or legends.

weeks. Schedules of parades are printed in the newspapers and local magazines.

Every parade has a theme chosen by the krewe. Each float carries out the theme. Like the plays at the ball, the themes are about events in history or famous legends and stories.

> Some huge floats are as tall as two-story buildings.

Most of the floats are pulled by trucks. Long ago, the floats were built on top of wooden wagons. Horses pulled the wagons through the streets. People carrying torches walked alongside to light up the float. Today many floats are covered with neon lights. Others have moving parts. Some huge floats are as tall as two-story buildings.

The float that carries the king and queen is always special. The most famous king is Rex. He waves to the crowds from his bandwagon. His attendants are dressed in purple, green, and gold. These are the colors of Mardi Gras.

Some krewes, such as Bacchus, choose a famous person like a television or movie star to be their parade's king. Dukes and maids dressed in costumes ride in another float behind the king's float.

A parade might have twenty or more floats. There are also lots of marching bands. Larger parades may have as many as sixty different bands marching with them. The Rex parade, one of the largest in New Orleans, may have more than three thousand people riding in floats and marching. Parades last from two to four hours. All of the parades can be watched for free.

The king is riding on a special float during this parade.

These children are holding their own Mardi Gras parade at a school in Houston, Texas, in 2006. They were not able to go home to New Orleans because of Hurricane Katrina.

Krewe members pay for the cost of building the floats and for their costumes. They also spend thousands of dollars on souvenirs. Souvenirs are things that people keep to remind them of special events. Mardi Gras souvenirs are called "throws" because the people riding the floats, called "maskers," throw them to the crowds. Popular throws are plastic-bead necklaces, plastic cups, and

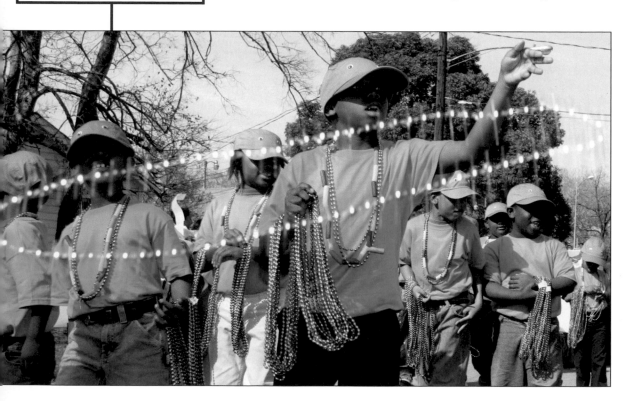

aluminum coins. The coins are stamped with the krewe's symbol on one side. The other side has the parade's theme.

These special coins are called "doubloons." They are named for Spanish gold pieces used in the 1500s. The first doubloon was thrown by Rex in 1960. Since then, krewes have stamped special coins each year to throw. Whether they are beads or coins, throws make Mardi Gras parades different from all other parades.

Every year it costs a lot of money to buy all the throws. In recent years, some krewes have stopped parading. Their members could no longer afford to pay for the floats and throws. But new krewes have started up and continue the tradition.

These are some of the doubloons that are thrown to the crowds during a Mardi Gras parade. They say "Happy Mardi Gras."

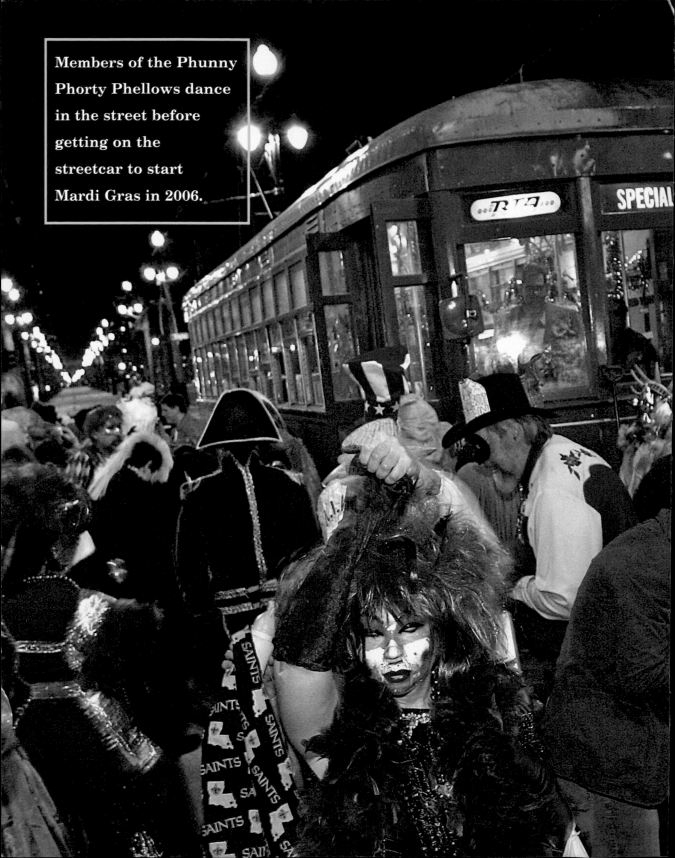

Members of the Phunny Phorty Phellows dance in the street before getting on the streetcar to start Mardi Gras in 2006.

CARNIVAL

THE CARNIVAL SEASON BEGINS ON TWELFTH Night, or January 6. Each year one of the krewes in New Orleans, called the Phunny Phorty Phellows, rides in a streetcar on January 6. A sign on the side announces, "It's Carnival Time."

In the evening, many people attend large balls. They wear fancy clothes with masks or costumes. Everyone loves going to carnival parties. A popular tradition is eating King Cakes. King Cakes look like

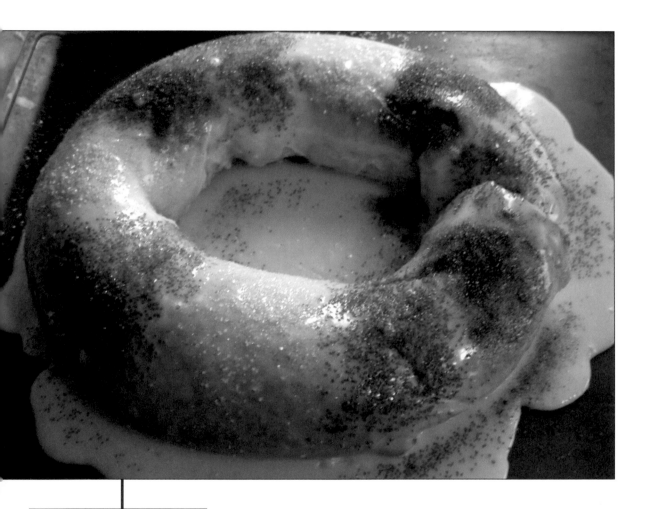

This king cake is decorated with the three colors of Mardi Gras—purple, green, and gold.

large oval doughnuts. They are decorated with purple, green, and gold icing. Most of the cakes contain a small doll. The doll symbolizes the baby Jesus who was visited by the Three Wise Men on January 6. Whoever finds the small doll has to help host the next party or buy the next cake. Some cakes have a small golden bean in them instead of a doll.

King Cake parties are very popular. More than half a million King Cakes are eaten every year in New Orleans. In Biloxi, Mississippi, bakers start baking King Cakes as soon as Christmas is over. They want to be sure that they will have enough made when carnival begins.

> More than half a million King Cakes are eaten every year in New Orleans.

As the time draws closer to Mardi Gras, there are more events. Cities have art exhibits, concerts, beauty pageants, stage shows, and costume contests. Galveston, Texas, has an annual rugby tournament. Rugby is a game similar to soccer and football. And, of course, every week brings more masked balls and parades. Excitement builds and builds.

Colorful masks and costumes are an important part of Mardi Gras celebrations, wherever they take place!

OTHER CELEBRATIONS

EVERY YEAR MORE CITIES ACROSS THE country are joining in the fun of Mardi Gras. The celebration in Mobile, Alabama, the oldest in our country, is similar to the one in New Orleans. However, instead of each secret club selecting a king and queen, there is only one king and queen for the whole celebration. The royal couple is chosen at a special ball on the Saturday before Mardi Gras. It is a great honor to be selected.

Mobile has another tradition that is different. Along with the plastic beads and trinkets, maskers throw moon pies at the crowd. Moon pies are round and about four inches wide. They are named after the company that first made them. The pies look like cakes. They are filled with cream and covered with chocolate icing. Each pie is wrapped in clear plastic.

About 250,000 moon pies are thrown each day during the last two weeks of carnival.

At one time, maskers threw boxes of Cracker Jack. The parade organizers were afraid someone might be hurt. Cracker Jack was banned as a throw. The maskers wanted to throw some other kind of food. That is when they started using moon pies. It is believed that the first moon pie was thrown in the Comic Cowboys' parade in 1953.

People along the parade route try to catch the pies as they are tossed from the floats. Some societies have special moon pies in different flavors. Some pies are banana or cherry flavored. The special pies are wrapped in silver paper. The club emblem is stamped on the wrapper.

It is estimated that two hundred fifty thousand moon pies are thrown each day during the last two weeks of carnival. The maskers also throw pieces of hard candy and bags of popcorn or peanuts.

Galveston, Texas, has many events during the carnival season. There are lots of parades, beauty pageants, art exhibits, and balls. On the Sunday before Mardi Gras, the annual Munchkin Parade takes place. Children ages four to fourteen

Moon pies are a popular Mardi Gras treat in Mobile, Alabama. Maskers throw them to the crowd during parades.

These girls are running in a pancake race in Liberal, Kansas.

dress in costumes and ride on decorated floats. After the parade, the Galveston Symphony presents a children's concert.

On the day of Mardi Gras, Galveston carries on the traditions of Pancake Tuesday started in England. There are pancake-eating and pancake-flipping contests, pancake races, and a pancake cook-off.

Mardi Gras is celebrated in many other cities in the United States and around the world. Two of the biggest celebrations outside of the U.S. are in

A parade-goer in Rio de Janeiro, Brazil, dresses as French king Louis XIV, also known as "the Sun King."

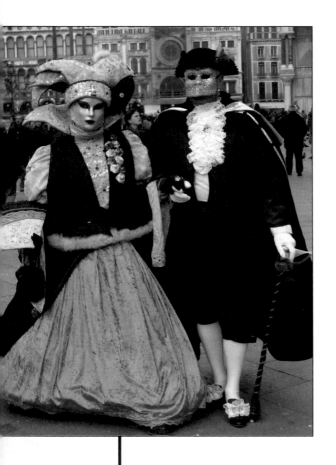

People dress up in beautifully decorated costumes to celebrate carnival in Venice, Italy.

Brazil and in Venice, Italy, where it is called carnival.

Many events copy things done in New Orleans. There are gumbo cook-offs. Gumbo is a meat or seafood stew made with vegetables. It is popular in New Orleans. People taste each gumbo entry and choose the one they like best.

Musicians play Dixieland music. Other entertainers sing and dance for the audience. Finally it is time for the parade. Krewes and businessmen from the local area have built the floats. Forty to fifty floats roll down the street. Children and adults crowd as close as they can, hoping to catch some beads. After the parade, there is a costume ball and dinner.

In other places, neighborhoods, and small communities, people put on their own Mardi Gras parades. Families work together to build the floats. Children dress in costumes. Boy Scouts and Girl Scouts march in the parade. High-school bands play music. Everyone has a great time.

These men are playing instruments in the 2007 "Krewe du Vieux" parade in New Orleans.

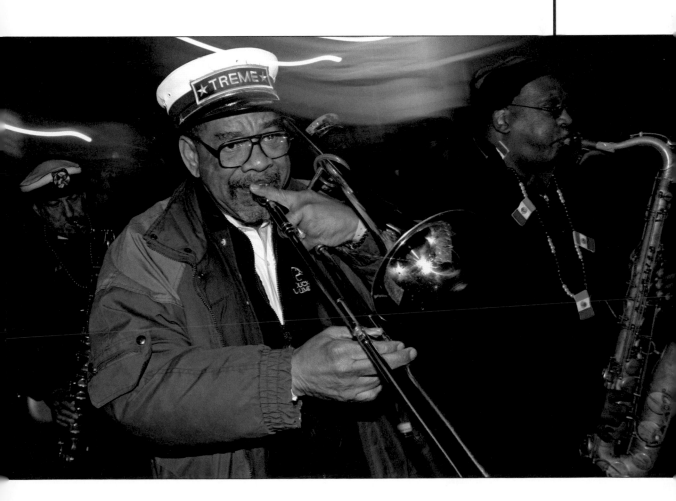

MARDI GRAS IN CANADA

MANY CITIES IN CANADA CELEBRATE CARNIVAL season and Mardi Gras. French explorers settled in parts of Canada and brought Mardi Gras with them. Several cities combine Mardi Gras celebrations with winter sports games. Edmonton, Alberta, has a Muk-Luk Mardi Gras. This is the city's winter sports carnival.

The most famous carnival and Mardi Gras is held in Quebec City. Quebec held its first celebration in 1864. The people welcomed the celebration. They loved having a break from the long harsh winter.

Every year since 1955, Quebec has held their "Carnaval de Quebec" (Carnival of Quebec). It lasts for seventeen days. It is the world's third-largest carnival after Rio de Janeiro in South America and New Orleans.

The crowds welcome Bonhomme to Quebec in 2006.

Just like the carnival season in the United States, there are lots of King Cake parties, balls, and parades. But there are also many winter activities that take place outside. There are snow sculpture contests, ice canoe races across the St. Lawrence River, and Roll in the Snow events.

In 1994, more than 1 million people took part in Quebec's carnival. The symbol

These men are ready to start the Quebec Winter Carnival ice canoe race in 2007.

of Quebec's carnival is Bonhomme, a snowman. In the beginning of January, Bonhomme arrives. The mayor of the city welcomes Bonhomme. He gives Bonhomme the "key" to the city. This is a symbol that Bonhomme is in charge of the city during carnival. A young woman is chosen to be carnival queen.

Each year an ice palace is built for Bonhomme. The palace is made from snow. It takes more than nine thousand tons of ice and snow to make the palace. Fifteen men work every day for about two months. When it is finished, the ice palace is seventy-five feet tall. It becomes the main attraction of carnival. Tourists love to visit the palace and take pictures of it.

People wear costumes to the annual Mardi Gras Ball. The highlight of the season is the Mardi Gras parade. The brightly lit parade has beautiful floats, clowns, and bands. More than half a million people bundle up in warm clothes to watch. As carnival and Mardi Gras end, Bonhomme returns the key to the city. He bids farewell until the next year's celebration.

The crowds are admiring Bonhomme's ice castle.

MARDI GRAS FUN

MARDI GRAS IS NOT MEANT TO BE SERIOUS. The purpose of the holiday is to have fun. People love to wear costumes and act silly.

Instead of white horses, mules lead the king's float in the Sparta parade in New Orleans. Comus holds a goblet instead of a royal scepter.

The theme song of Mardi Gras in New Orleans is a silly song called "If Ever I Cease to Love." The first verse says:

If ever I cease to love,
If ever I cease to love,
May oysters have legs,
And cows lay eggs,
If ever I cease to love.

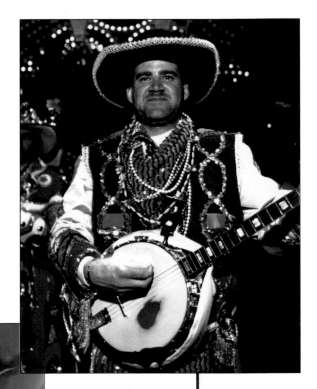

This parade marcher is dressed up as a cowboy.

Dogs in New Orleans have their own parade, and their very own krewe—the Mystic Krewe of Barkus.

MARDI GRAS ARRIVES

AFTER WEEKS OF BALLS AND PARADES, MARDI Gras is here. On Tuesday morning in New Orleans, people are up early. Many dress in costumes. Some have worked on their costumes for many months, sewing on feathers and sequins. Everyone enjoys playing make-believe. Soon the sidewalks are lined with costumed people waiting for the parades.

Parades start as early as 8:00 A.M. There may be as many as five or more throughout the day. Thousands of tourists come from all over the world to take part in the day's merrymaking. Some people bring stepladders to stand on so they can get a better view of the floats. Others spread out blankets and eat picnic lunches while they wait.

Street vendors push carts and sell funny items like blinking bow ties, fake noses, and glowing necklaces. Others sell popcorn, cotton candy, and other treats. Musicians are everywhere, playing and marching through the crowd.

Everyone wants souvenir throws from the floats. Bead necklaces are the most common. But the maskers also throw Frisbees™ and other small plastic toys. A few lucky people will catch a

The Golden Eagles African-American Indian tribe parades in their decorative hand-made costumes in 2006.

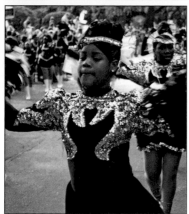

Marching bands participate in many parades throughout New Orleans.

gold-colored doubloon stamped with the carnival's symbol.

While waiting for a parade, the crowds hope to see the Mardi Gras Indians. "Tribes" of Mardi Gras Indians have marched for more than one hundred years. No one knows how they began, but members are African Creoles (people of mixed African, American Indian, French, and Spanish descent).

The Mardi Gras Indians march through neighborhoods dancing to music. They do not have a set parade route and can appear anywhere. Mardi Gras Indians wear beautiful costumes covered with thousands of beads, sequins, rhinestones, and feathers. All of the designs of flowers or animals are sewn by hand. Some of the costumes take months to make. They are worn only once. As the Mardi Gras Indians pass by, many people join in behind dancing to the rhythm of their tunes.

Another favorite parade is put on by the Zulu krewe. Zulu is the oldest African-American krewe. They began marching in 1909. The Zulu parade is held early in the morning. Many of their maskers wear grass skirts. A lucky person in the crowd might catch a valuable throw—a decorated coconut, symbol of the Zulus.

The streets and sidewalks overflow with people laughing, singing, and dancing. In the evening, after the last parade, the final costume balls are held. At midnight, police blow horns. The horns let people know that it is time to go home. Mardi Gras is over. Street sweepers begin cleaning up the tons of leftover confetti, plastic cups, and beads.

Mardi Gras Indians wear beautiful costumes covered with thousands of beads, sequins, rhinestones, and feathers.

A King and Queen ride by on their float during the 2006 Zulu krewe parade.

This year's Mardi Gras is already a memory. But in a few days, the krewes will be busy planning next year's themes and floats. Everyone looks forward to the season of the year when people of all races and backgrounds come together for the magic that is Mardi Gras.

WORDS TO KNOW

Ash Wednesday—The first day of Lent. Lent is the six-week period before Easter.

ball—A fancy party.

carnival—The days from January 6 until Mardi Gras that are filled with parties and parades.

doubloon—A Spanish gold coin used a long time ago.

emblem—A symbol or design that represents something, such as a company or a special club.

fast—To not eat food or to eat only small amounts of food.

King Cakes—Special cakes baked during carnival season. They contain a small doll or bean. Whoever finds the doll must give the next party.

krewe—The name for secret clubs that plan Mardi Gras parades and balls.

Lent—A six-week time of preparation for Easter.

maskers—Costumed float riders.

souvenirs—Something kept as a reminder of a person, place, or event.

tableau—A play performed at a ball by krewe members.

theme—The main idea or subject of something.

throws—Souvenirs tossed to the crowds from the Mardi Gras floats.

tradition—To do the same thing in the same way every year.

LEARN MORE

Books

Flanagan, Alice K. *Carnival*. Minneapolis: Compass Point Books, 2004.

Foran, Jill. *Mardi Gras*. Mankato, Minn.: Weigl Publishers, 2003.

Heinrichs, Ann. *Mardi Gras*. Chanhassen, Minn.: Child's World, 2006.

Internet Addresses

Mardi Gras
http://www.activityvillage.co.uk/mardi_gras.htm

MardiGrasDay.com
http://www.mardigrasday.com/

Mardi Gras on the Net
http://www.holidays.net/mardigras/

INDEX